For John and Jack M.R.

For Nicola and Gilean M.M.

OXFORD
UNIVERSITY PRESS

Great Clarendon Street, Oxford OX2 6DP

Oxford   New York

Athens Auckland Bangkok Bogotá Buenos Aires Calcutta
Cape Town Chennai Dar es Salaam Delhi Florence Hong Kong Istanbul
Karachi Kuala Lumpur Madrid Melbourne Mexico City Mumbai
Nairobi Paris São Paulo Singapore Taipei Tokyo Toronto Warsaw
and associated companies in
Berlin   Ibadan

Oxford is a trade mark of Oxford University Press

Text copyright © Marion Rose 1999
Illustrations copyright © Moira Maclean 1999

First published 1999

Marion Rose and Moira Maclean have asserted their moral
right to be known as the authors of the work.

ISBN 0 19 279016 1 (hardback)
ISBN 0 19 272336 7 (paperback)

Printed in Hong Kong

Sssh! The Moon is Sleeping

Marion Rose

Illustrated by Moira Maclean

OXFORD
UNIVERSITY PRESS

Sssh! The moon is sleeping,
See her soft and dreamy look?
Now it's other people's bedtimes.
You can see them in this book.

Here's a girl with just one slipper
And a dressing gown that's torn.
Her two bossy older sisters
Are out discoing till dawn.

She's quite happy, sipping cocoa,
Chatting to her Fairy 'Mum.
Soon she'll be asleep and dreaming,
Dreaming that her prince will come.

Three pink brothers in the bathtub,
Hear them grumble, grunt, and groan!
They've been working hard all day to
Finish off their house of stone.

Come and see—at last it's ready!
They are safe and sound indoors!
Soon the empty streets will echo
With their happy, piggy snores.

Look what's happening in Bear Cottage
(That's the house up on the heath).
Baby Bear is busy brushing
Bits of porridge from his teeth!

Mum and Dad are sitting looking
At their unexpected guest.
It's a sleepy blonde-haired burglar
Who came in—and took a rest!

What a noisy bedtime game is
Coming from that bungalow!
Who began a pillow fight with
Seven short men in a row?

One is snoring, one is sniffing,
One's complaining with a frown.
One is grinning, one is blushing.
Will they ever settle down!

Listen! There is someone singing,
Singing sadly—soft and sweet.
See—her long and lovely hair falls
Like a river to the street.

Every day her wicked jailer
Scrambles up without a care.
Swish, swish! Can you hear her brushing
All the tangles from her hair?

This boy lives with his poor mother.
Just today he sold their cow!
She got mad and threw the beans out …
Something's out there, growing, NOW!

There… it's winding past his window!
On and on and up it goes.
When he wakes he'll find a beanstalk!
(Magic happens while you doze.)

Follow me into the forest
(Watch your feet and mind your head).
See this house that's made of sugar?
Here a witch is going to bed.

First she takes her pointed hat off,
Guzzles frogs, puts out the cat.
Now she hangs beside her broomstick—
Upside down! Imagine that!

Here's another who's dead weary.
She's run right across the wood,
Told her mum a scary story
Of a wolf who is no good.

Now she's snug in her pyjamas,
Tucked up safely in her bed.
Click! She puts her bedside light out
For she's such a sleepy head!

In the castle on the hilltop
Sleeps a princess young and fair.
All around her, lords and ladies
Slumber deeply everywhere.

In her hand she holds a spindle
And her dreams are all of this:
That a prince will gently wake her
In the morning, with a kiss.

Sssh! The moon is sleeping,
Cow has made her great big leap.
Cat and fiddle are both snoring.
Everyone is fast asleep.

One last light shines in the darkness
Miles and miles away it's true.
Someone's still awake and peeping . . .
Bless my whiskers! Is it YOU?